Copyright © 2021 Clavis Publishing Inc., New York

Originally published as *Luuk en Lotje. Het is winter!* in Belgium
and the Netherlands by Clavis Uitgeverij, 2016
English translation from the Dutch by Clavis Publishing Inc., New York

Visit us on the Web at www.clavis-publishing.com.

Luke and Lottie. Winter Is Here! written and illustrated by Ruth Wielockx

ISBN 978-1-60537-696-7

This book was printed in July 2021 at Wai Man Book Binding (China) Ltd. Flat A, 9/F., Phase 1,
Kwun Tong Industrial Centre, 472-484 Kwun Tong Road, Kwun Tong, Kowloon, H.K.

First Edition
10 9 8 7 6 5 4 3 2 1

Clavis Publishing supports the First Amendment and celebrates the right to read.

Ruth Wielockx

Luke and Lottie

Winter Is Here!

Clavis
NEW YORK

Winter is here!
Luke and Lottie are going to play in the garden.
They put on warm coats, gloves, and winter boots.
"Don't forget your hat, Luke!" says Lottie.
"You have to wear so many clothes in the winter,"
Luke grumbles.

Brrr, it's cold outside.
When Luke and Lottie talk, a small cloud comes out of their mouths
Lottie carefully carries a bowl of water to the birdhouse.
"Do you have food for the birds, Luke?" she asks.

"The birds are having a party!"
Luke cheers, waving the streamer
of peanuts. Ooh! It's raining peanuts!

Suddenly Luke stops.
"Look," he calls out surprised. "Cotton is falling from the sky."
Lottie giggles. "That's not cotton, those are snowflakes."
"I'm going to count all the flakes," says Luke. "One, two . . ."
". . . many!" Lottie shrieks.

"So much snow . . ." says Luke with a sigh.
"Enough snow to make a snowman!" Lottie says excitedly.
Luke and Lottie first make a small ball.
The snow is nice and sticky and the ball is getting bigger and bigger .

Look! The snowman is done!
He has a carrot for a nose
and pebbles for a mouth.

"Something is missing." Luke runs inside.
Oh! Mom's pretty hat!
"Now it's a snow lady," Luke chuckles.
Luckily Dad brings the sled and an old hat from the shed.

"Go, horsie, go!" Lottie yells.
Luke is pulling the sled. But then he gets tired.
"Now you have to be the horse," Luke says.
"No, you're the horse," says Lottie.
But Luke runs away. And then . . .

Smack! A snowball lands on Lottie.
Smack! And another one!
The snowballs fly back and forth.
It's a real snowball fight!

It's getting dark outside. It's snowing softly.
Luke and Lottie are sitting cozy inside.
They're drinking hot chocolate. Yummy, that's good!
"Winter is so much fun," Lottie says.
"Shall we go play in the snow again tomorrow, Luke? Luke…"